For Mailee and her grandchildren — J.O.
For Jason x — Lindsey

OXFORD
UNIVERSITY PRESS

Great Clarendon Street, Oxford OX2 6DP
Oxford University Press is a department of the University of Oxford.
It furthers the University's objective of excellence in research, scholarship,
and education by publishing worldwide in

Oxford   New York

Auckland Cape Town Dar es Salaam Hong Kong Karachi
Kuala Lumpur Madrid Melbourne Mexico City Nairobi
New Delhi Shanghai Taipei Toronto

With offices in

Argentina Austria Brazil Chile Czech Republic France Greece
Guatemala Hungary Italy Japan Poland Portugal Singapore
South Korea Switzerland Thailand Turkey Ukraine Vietnam

Oxford is a registered trade mark of Oxford University Press
in the UK and in certain other countries

First published in 2009

British Library Cataloguing in Publication

Data available

ISBN: 978-0-19-279170-2 (Hardback)
ISBN: 978-0-19-279171-9 (Paperback)
ISBN: 978-0-19-279246-4 (Paperback with audio CD)

1 3 5 7 9 10 8 6 4 2

Printed in China

Paper used in the production of this book is a natural,
recyclable product made from wood grown in sustainable forests.
The manufacturing process conforms to the environmental
regulations of the country of origin.

Over in the Clover

Jan
Ormerod

OXFORD
UNIVERSITY PRESS

Lindsey
Gardiner

Over in the **forest**, in a cave so snug,
one cubby bear gives his mummy a hug.

'Hug!' says the mummy.
'I hug!' says the one.
And they snuggle, buggle, hug
in their cave so snug.

Over in the jungle, in a leafy glade, two stripy tigers tumble in the shade.

'Roll!' says the daddy.
'We roll!' say the two.

And they jungle, bungle, tumble
in their shady glade.

Over in the clover, in the bright moonlight, three baby moles burrow through the night.

'Dig!' says the mummy.

'We dig!' say the three.

And they doggle, daggle, dig in the bright moonlight.

Over by the river,
at the trunk of a tree,
four busy beavers
chew noisily.

Over in the clouds, on a mountain crest,
six fluffy eagles **flap** in a nest.

'Flap!' says the daddy. 'We flap!' say the six.

And they flip, flap, fly from their nest on a crest.

Over in the desert, by a dusty pool,
seven little warthogs try to keep cool.

'Snuffle!' says the mummy.

'We snuffle!' say the seven.

And they **shuffle,** **wuffle,** **snuffle** by the **dusty** pool.

Over in the garden,
where it's lovely and warm,

eight pretty kitties
s t r e t c h
paws on the lawn.

'Stretch!' says the daddy.
'We stretch!'
say the eight.

And
they
furry, purry,
s t r e t c h

on the
lawn in the
warm.

Over in the park, on a grassy mound,
nine puppy dogs
chase round
and round.

'Run!' says the mummy.

'We run!' say the nine.

And they
yip,

yap,

run

as they **race** round the mound.

Over in the **fishpond**,
underneath
a log,

ten tiny tadpoles
waiting to be frogs!

'Wiggle!'
says the daddy.

'We wiggle!'
say the ten.

And they wiggle, waggle, woggle
underneath a log, and wiggle into . . .

frogs!

1 one cubby bear

2 two stripy tigers

3 three baby moles

4 four busy beavers

5 five kangaroos

6   six fluffy eagles

7   seven little warthogs

8   eight pretty kitties

9   nine puppy dogs

10   ten tiny tadpoles